GHOSTS IN GRIZZLY MANSION!

Something strange is going on at Grizzly Mansion. Everyone hears mysterious noises at night. Then Maisie the cook sees ghosts in the ballroom. And now Lady Grizzly's prize antiques are starting to disappear. It looks like the family curse might be real after all—which means Bad Bart Grizzly has returned from beyond the grave!

THE MANIAC OF GRIZZLY MANSION!

The Berenstain Bears in MANIAC MANSION

by the Berenstains

A BIG CHAPTER BOOK™

Random House 🏠 New York

Copyright © 1996 by Berenstain Enterprises, Inc.

http://www.randomhouse.com/

Library of Congress Cataloging-in-Publication Data
Berenstain, Stan.
The Berenstain Bears in maniac mansion /
by the Berenstains.
    p.   cm. — (Big chapter book)
SUMMARY: When priceless antiques begin to disappear from Squire
Grizzly's mansion, the ghost of his ancestor Bad Bart is suspected.
ISBN 0-679-88156-5 (trade) — ISBN 0-679-98156-X (lib. bdg.)
[1. Bears—Fiction.   2. Ghosts—Fiction.
3. Mystery and detective stories.]   I. Berenstain, Jan, 1923– .
II. Title.   III. Series: Berenstain, Stan, 1923– Big chapter books.
PZ7.B4483Beri   1996
[Fic]—dc20
96-5452

Printed in the United States of America   10 9 8 7 6 5 4 3 2

BIG CHAPTER BOOKS is a trademark of Berenstain Enterprises, Inc.

Contents

Chapter 1
Mansion Mishap

Papa Q. Bear was known far and wide as one of the finest carpenters in all Bear Country. That meant that he always had plenty of customers. In fact, he usually had a waiting list as long as your arm.

But Papa had one special customer who was always at the top of his list. That customer was Squire Grizzly. Because Papa was the best carpenter in Beartown, Squire and Lady Grizzly wouldn't let anyone else take care of the woodwork at Grizzly Mansion.

Over the years Papa had probably done more work for the Grizzlys than for all his other customers put together. That was partly because Grizzly Mansion had so much woodwork. The mansion had dozens of rooms, and in every room there was woodwork on the walls and ceiling. There were also lots of stairways in Grizzly Mansion. Each stairway had wooden steps that sometimes needed repair and also finely carved banisters that had to be cleaned and refinished from time to time. Papa had even replaced damaged banisters on several of the stairways.

But an even bigger job than Grizzly Mansion's woodwork was its furniture. Lady Grizzly was a collector of fine old furniture. Every room of the mansion was filled with priceless antiques she had bought over the

years. Each time she bought one, she gave it to Papa Bear to take apart, clean, put back together, and refinish. If it was damaged in any way, Papa would repair it with the utmost care.

There were two reasons Papa took such great care with the antiques from Grizzly Mansion. First, he always took pride in his work. And second, he knew how much Lady Grizzly loved her antiques. The squire spoke often of how upset she got when even one of them had so much as a scratch.

Papa wasn't at all surprised, then, to hear the panic in Squire Grizzly's voice over the phone one summer afternoon.

"I *broke* it!" said the squire. "One of her favorite rosewood chairs! I've put on a little weight recently, and I must have sat down too hard on it. If she sees it, she'll have a fit. Oh, if I'd only gone on that diet she's been pestering me about!"

"Don't worry, Squire," said Papa. "I can start work on the chair first thing tomorrow morning and bring it back after lunch. Should I come to one of the side doors to pick it up so Lady Grizzly won't see me and wonder why I'm there?"

"Don't bother sneaking around," said the squire. "Lady Grizzly's still asleep."

"I hope she isn't ill," said Papa.

"Oh, no. She hasn't been able to sleep at night lately. I'll tell you all about it when you get here. Greeves the butler will show you to my office."

Papa told Mama what had happened and headed out to the family car. But first he called upstairs to Brother, Sister, and Cousin Fred, who was visiting for the afternoon.

The cubs always enjoyed going along with

Papa on his trips to Grizzly Mansion. The grounds were so beautiful, especially in the summer. And the mansion itself was full of interesting things to look at, such as old suits of armor and huge portraits of Grizzly forebears.

For Brother there was the added attraction of Bonnie Brown, his special friend. Bonnie was the Grizzlys' niece. Her parents were in show business and were away from home most of the time. Sometimes Bonnie was in a play or show, too. The rest of the time she lived at Grizzly Mansion with her aunt and uncle.

The cubs hurried downstairs and piled into the car. Papa started it up, and off they went to Grizzly Mansion.

Chapter 2
A Bad Lot

Arriving at Grizzly Mansion was different from arriving at any other house. First Papa and the cubs had to stop at the front gate and report to the security guard on duty there.

"Papa Q. Bear to see Squire Grizzly," said Papa.

"Greeves just buzzed me on the intercom and told me to expect you, Papa," said the guard. "Drive right in."

Papa steered the car up the long drive-

way and around the circle at its end. When Greeves greeted Papa and the cubs at the front door, they noticed that he had large bags under his eyes.

"You look tired, Greeves," said Papa. "Anything wrong?"

"Not really, sir," said the butler. "I just haven't been sleeping well lately."

Hmm, thought Papa. *Just like Lady Grizzly. Maybe it's catching.*

They entered the front hallway that led to the main spiral staircase. As the cubs admired a suit of armor that stood before several life-size portraits of Grizzly forebears, Greeves went to an intercom and pressed a button. "The cubs have arrived, Miss Bonnie," he said.

Bonnie waved as she came skipping down the stairs. "Hi, guys," she said. "How about a tour of the mansion?"

"Great," said Brother. "I've never been upstairs. Can we go up and look around?"

"Sure," said Bonnie, taking his hand. "Let's go."

Once upstairs, Bonnie led the cubs down a long hallway lined with portraits.

"Wow," said Sister. "How many forebears do the Grizzlys have, anyway?"

"Dozens," said Bonnie. "The family goes back centuries."

Brother stopped in front of one of the portraits. It was of a very old white-haired

bear who looked out from the canvas with dark beady eyes. The eyes had an odd gleam in them. Brother had a hunch that the gleam was a greedy one.

"Who's this old guy?" he asked Bonnie. "I don't think I like the looks of him."

"Funny you should say that," said Bonnie. "That's old Farnsworth Grizzly, Uncle Squire's great-grandfather. He built Grizzly Mansion, you know. And he was definitely *not* a nice bear."

"What did he do that wasn't nice?" asked Sister.

9

"He was a dishonest gambler—a swindler. He cheated bears out of tons of money."

"Kind of an old-time Ralph Ripoff," said Brother.

"But much, much worse," said Bonnie. "Farnsworth Grizzly made Ralph look like an honest citizen. Ralph still lives in that run-down houseboat, but Farnsworth Grizzly swindled his way into a mansion."

"I never knew your uncle's family had such a bad apple in its barrel," said Brother.

"It wasn't just Farnsworth," said Bonnie. "The old-time Grizzlys were a bad lot. Farnsworth was the last of the bad ones, but he was far from the worst."

"Who was the worst?" asked Cousin Fred.

"Follow me and I'll show you," said Bonnie.

She led them to the very end of the hall, where a large portrait hung high on the wall. It was a painting of a very mean-looking bear dressed in what might have been pirates' clothes. He wore a black wide-brimmed hat with a feather in it and a black waistcoat with huge gold buttons. In one side of his belt was tucked an old-fashioned pistol; in the other was an antique dagger. Across his eyes stretched a black mask, and his mouth was twisted into a snarl.

"Is *that* a Grizzly?" asked Sister, staring up at the portrait.

"The very first one," said Bonnie. "He was an orphan, and no one knows who his parents were. Have you guys ever heard of Bad Bart Grizzly?"

"The Maniac of Mountain Highway?" said Cousin Fred. "You mean *he* was related to the squire?"

"That's the only reason he's here on the wall," said Bonnie.

"Who was he?" asked Sister.

"He was a famous highway robber from centuries ago," said Fred. "He and his band of thieves used to rob stagecoaches along Old Mountain Highway in the Great Grizzly Mountains. It was just called Mountain Highway in those days."

"Like Robin Bear of Bearwood Forest?" asked Sister.

"Not exactly," said Bonnie. "Robin Bear robbed from the rich and gave to the poor. Bad Bart robbed from the rich, stole from the poor—and kept everything for himself! He didn't just rob travelers, either. At night he would break into the cottages of the poor mountain folk, scare them out of their wits, and take everything they owned. That's why they called him a maniac."

Sister looked up at the portrait again and shivered. "Can we go back downstairs now?" she said. "It's kind of creepy up here."

Cousin Fred groaned. But Brother was feeling protective toward his little sister. "Come on, Sis," he said. "We'll go see the ballroom instead."

As they passed the portrait of Farnsworth Grizzly on their way to the stairs, Brother suddenly felt Sister's hand on his arm. "What's wrong, Sis?" he said.

She glanced over her shoulder at the portrait. "Is that a trick painting?" she asked.

"What do you mean?" said Bonnie.

"The eyes followed me as I went past!" said Sister.

Brother chuckled and put his arm around Sister's shoulders as they went down the stairs. "Isn't it amazing what your imagination can do when you're scared?" he said.

Chapter 3
Farnsworth Grizzly's Curse

Meanwhile, in Squire Grizzly's office, Papa and the squire were also talking about Grizzly forebears. The conversation turned in that direction when Papa asked the squire why Lady Grizzly and Greeves were having trouble sleeping.

"You wouldn't believe what's been going on around here the last couple of weeks," said the squire, shaking his head. "And all because of that silly old curse."

"What curse?" asked Papa.

"The curse put on the mansion by

my great-grandfather Farnsworth Grizzly," said the squire. "When my grandfather, Farnsworth's son, turned his back on crime and became an honest banker, Farnsworth was furious. He said that Bad Bart Grizzly must be turning over in his grave, and he predicted that someday Bad Bart's ghost would come to haunt Grizzly Mansion.

"I never told my wife about the curse, because I know she believes in ghosts, and I didn't want to frighten her. But she found out about it from one of the history books in my study. She got all upset. Then she told the servants, and *they* got all upset.

"A couple of weeks ago they started hearing noises at night and wondered if the ghost of Bad Bart had finally come to haunt the mansion. A few nights later Maisie, the cook, heard noises coming from the ballroom in the west wing. She got out of bed and peeked into the ballroom. She claims that she saw three figures. Two of them were carrying a table across the room, and the third was walking ahead of them, lighting their way with a candle."

"Burglars?" said Papa.

"Nonsense," said the squire. "She says the figures were wearing masks and outfits like the ones worn by highway robbers in olden times. And remember, the leader carried a candle instead of a flashlight. Obviously, she imagined it all. She expected to see the ghosts of Bad Bart and his thieves in that ballroom, so that's exactly what she saw. Since she knew they were thieves, she imagined them stealing something.

"I checked the ballroom the next morning and found nothing missing. Every piece of furniture was exactly where it should be. That *proves* it was just her imagination."

"And now no one can sleep at night listening for ghosts?" said Papa.

"All but Bonnie and me," said the squire. "I know it's nonsense, and I've forbidden the others from telling Bonnie about it. I don't want her young mind disturbed with such silliness. But my wife sleeps most of the day now, and Greeves and Maisie and Tillie the housekeeper are all so tired they can hardly do their jobs. Why, it takes forever to get a cup of tea around here now..."

Squire Grizzly rang the cook's buzzer and shouted at the top of his lungs, "Maisie, where is our tea?"

"What about the noise at night?" asked Papa.

"Oh, it's just mice running around all those secret tunnels that Farnsworth Grizzly built into the mansion—tunnels and stairways and hidden rooms with hidden entrances. He used to hide his money in them. From time to time he'd sneak around in them to switch the hiding places. He was a strange one, that Farnsworth Grizzly."

There was a knock at the door, and a very tired Maisie appeared. She was carrying a tray with two cups on it. "I'm sorry it took so long, sir," she told the squire. "I'm so tired that I seem to be doing everything in slow motion."

"More noises in the west wing last night?" asked the squire.

Maisie nodded and put a hand to her mouth to cover a yawn.

"Must be the Maniac of Mountain Highway," scoffed Squire Grizzly.

"Oh, we don't call him that anymore, sir," said Maisie. "Lady Grizzly says it's out of date."

"Oh?" said the squire. "And what do you call him now?"

"The Maniac of Grizzly Mansion!" said Maisie.

Squire Grizzly rolled his eyes at Papa as Maisie turned and trudged wearily from the room.

THE MANIAC OF
GRIZZLY MANSION

Chapter 4
Sister's Nightmare

Papa Bear knew very well that Sister was sometimes frightened by ghost stories and other scary tales. But on the way home from Grizzly Mansion, he couldn't help telling the cubs about Farnsworth Grizzly's curse and what Maisie thought she had seen in the ballroom.

"Now don't tell Bonnie about it when we take the chair back tomorrow," he added. "The squire doesn't want to scare her."

"Bonnie isn't scared of ghosts," said Brother. "She doesn't believe in them."

"I don't believe in ghosts, either," said Sister. "But they scare me anyway."

"Uh-oh," said Papa. "I hope you're not too scared to go back to the mansion with us tomorrow."

"Oh, no," said Sister. "I'll be okay...I think."

But that night something happened that almost convinced Sister not to return to Grizzly Mansion. She had a nightmare about it.

In dreams, even good ones, things often look strange and events happen in odd ways. Sister's dream was no exception. She

found herself on the lawn of Grizzly Mansion's west wing, watching Bonnie jump rope. "Ten thousand and two, ten thousand and three...," Bonnie was calling out.

It was strange that after so many jumps Bonnie didn't look the least bit tired. And it was also strange that it was the middle of the night. But strange as it all was, it seemed perfectly natural to Sister, the way things so often seem in dreams.

The mansion grounds were lit only by a full moon. But it wasn't very dark, because the moon was at least twice its normal size. So was the lawn. It stretched for what seemed like a mile off toward Grizzly Mansion. The mansion looked tiny in the distance.

All of a sudden Sister felt something tug at her. She began to glide across the lawn toward the mansion. She heard Bonnie's voice getting farther and farther away: "...fifteen thousand and eight, fifteen thousand and nine..."

The mansion grew larger and larger, until at last Sister found herself standing at the side door to the west wing. The door was open. Inside was a long dark hallway. Sister felt her heart beat faster. She didn't want to go in. But she couldn't seem to help herself. Something made her feet move.

She walked into the mansion and down the hallway. The hallway was lined with huge portraits of Grizzly forebears. Even in the dark Sister could see their eyes following her as she walked.

She was headed toward a room at the end of the hallway. From the room came a dim glow. *What was in that room?* Sister didn't know, and she didn't want to find out. But

just the same, her feet carried her down the hallway and toward the room.

It seemed to take forever to get all the way down the hall. Sister had plenty of time to tell herself over and over, "I should turn back..." Her mind heard her mouth say it, but her feet didn't seem to hear. They just kept walking down the hallway.

Finally, she stood in the doorway of the room. She recognized it now. It was the great ballroom in the west wing. At the far end of the room stood a row of suits of armor that held swords, spears, and maces. One suit right in the middle of the row also held a lit candle.

Suddenly, the candle began to move toward Sister. She heard the clanking of metal as the suit of armor walked.

I have to get away! she thought. But

when she turned to run, she found she couldn't move. Her legs were as heavy as logs, and her feet felt as if they were nailed to the floor.

The candle got closer and closer. But now the clanking had stopped. For it was no longer a suit of armor that held the candle. It was a tall figure in a black wide-brimmed hat and a black waistcoat with big gold buttons...and a *mask*. It was the Maniac of Mountain Highway!

Now the other suits of armor had changed into highway robbers, too! Here they came, all in a row behind Bad Bart!

Sister let out a scream just as Bad Bart

reached out and *grabbed her shoulder*...

"Wake up, Sis!" said Brother. He was shaking her shoulder.

Sister opened her eyes and looked around. She was glad to see her own bedroom again.

"You screamed in your sleep," said Brother. "Must have been dreaming."

Sister told Brother about her nightmare. "Now I'm *definitely* not going with you and Papa to Grizzly Mansion tomorrow," she said.

"But it was just a bad dream, Sis," said

Brother. "Nothing scary is going to happen at the mansion tomorrow. It'll be broad daylight. I don't believe in ghosts, you know, but the ghosts I don't believe in only come out at night."

"Hmm," said Sister. "You might be right about that."

"Of course I am," said Brother. "Now go back to sleep."

But Sister couldn't sleep at first. It was too quiet. Every little creak of the tree house made her imagine highway robbers climbing along the branches toward the windows.

Then Brother started snoring loudly. Sister imagined that Brother's snoring was the sound of saws cutting through the branches. That made the highway robbers fall to the ground and run away.

And so, finally, Sister drifted off to sleep.

Chapter 5
Isn't It Obvious?

Sister still wasn't sure about going to Grizzly Mansion when Brother asked her the next morning after breakfast.

"Well, you don't have to decide right this minute," said Brother. "I'm sure Papa isn't finished fixing the chair yet. Let's go out to the workshop and see how he's doing."

The cubs found Papa kneeling on the floor with chair parts spread around him. He was frowning at something in his hand.

"What's wrong, Papa?" asked Brother. "Can't you fix it?"

"Oh, I can fix it—that'll be easy," said Papa. "The problem is, this chair is definitely *not* an antique."

"How can you tell?" asked Sister.

Papa held up a shiny screw. "This screw is brand-new," he said. "Made with modern machine tools."

"Maybe someone replaced the screws," Brother suggested.

Papa shook his head. "I remember working on this very chair a few years back when Lady Grizzly bought it," he said. "I took it apart, cleaned it, and refinished it. It had original hand-made screws. They were still good, so I used them again when I put the chair back together. I know for a fact that no one has worked on the chair since. Now, let's see…"

Papa picked up one of the legs and examined it. "Ah, you see?" he said. "It's a fake! Now that I look at it more closely, I can see that it was made with modern tools. It's hand-made, and it's a very nice piece of work. It looks just like the original. But it's definitely a copy. You see these screw holes? They were obviously made with an electric drill!"

"Wait a minute," said Sister with a frown. "How can an antique change into a fake?"

Brother laughed. "It didn't *change,* Sis," he said. "Someone must have stolen it and left a fake in its place!"

For a moment Sister kept frowning. Then her frown vanished, her mouth came open, and her eyes grew wide. "That means Maisie was right!" she cried. "She really did see the ghosts of Bad Bart and his bandits stealing furniture!"

"Now, Sis," said Papa. "That can't be true. I agree with Squire Grizzly. Maisie imagined the whole thing."

"You mean it's just a coincidence that an antique has been stolen?" said Sister.

"Er...uh...well, I...," said Papa. "Brother, explain it to your sister."

"Me?" said Brother. "Well, I...er...uh…"

"Never mind," said Papa. "The important thing is that we have to get right over to Grizzly Mansion and tell the squire!"

Sister took a step backward toward the workshop door. "That's okay," she said. "You guys can go without me."

"Come on, Sis!" said Brother. "You've got to go! Cousin Fred, too!"

"Oh, yeah?" said Sister. "Why?"

"Isn't it obvious?" said Brother. "This is a job for the *Bear Detectives!*"

Chapter 6
Strange Behavior

Papa and the cubs hurried over to Grizzly Mansion, stopping on the way to pick up Cousin Fred.

"Well, well, if it isn't Papa Bear," said the security guard at the front gate. "I wasn't expecting you until after lunch."

"Urgent business," said Papa.

When Greeves answered the front door,

his eyebrows went up. "Oh, it's you, sir," he said. "What can I do for you?"

"We need to see Squire Grizzly right away," said Papa. "Someone has stolen one of Lady Grizzly's priceless antiques!"

The butler's eyebrows raised even higher. "Oh, dear," he said. "That's awful. But I'm afraid the squire is not at home. He went to an early business meeting in town. He won't be back until after lunch."

"What about Lady Grizzly?" asked Papa.

"Oh, she's sound asleep, sir," said Greeves. "I couldn't possibly wake her. She's been under such a strain lately, you know. We all have."

"You're right, Greeves," said Papa. "We'll come back later." He turned to leave, but he stopped and looked at Greeves.

"Yes, sir?" said the butler.

"Oh, nothing," said Papa. "It's just that

you look much more rested. The bags under your eyes are gone. You must have finally gotten some sleep."

"Oh...er, yes," said Greeves. "I did much better last night, sir."

"That's good," said Papa. "Well, we'll see you after lunch."

"Good-bye, sir."

As Papa and the cubs walked back to the car, they heard Bonnie calling them. "Hey, guys! Over here!" She was jumping rope on the lawn by the east wing.

"Ninety-eight, ninety-nine, *a hundred*." Bonnie stopped jumping just as they reached her. "Sorry I didn't come over," she said. "I wanted to get to a hundred. Why are you leaving so soon? Didn't you just get here?"

Papa explained that Greeves had told them the squire was away.

"No, he's not," said Bonnie, frowning. "He's in the dining room finishing his breakfast. Boy, that Greeves has been acting strange lately. All the servants have. I guess it's because of that silly ghost business."

"We thought you didn't know about that," said Brother.

"It's impossible to live in this mansion without knowing," said Bonnie. "Auntie and the servants are always talking about it. Come on, I'll take you to Uncle Squire. We'll use the side door. It's quicker."

Chapter 7
Good News and Bad News

Squire Grizzly was sitting at the dining table in the east wing of the mansion, sipping a cup of coffee. Spread around the table were serving dishes half filled with pancakes, sausages, and potatoes.

"Good morning, sweetie," he said when he saw Bonnie. "Oh, it's Papa and the cubs. Would you join me for breakfast? I'll ring Greeves for more juice and coffee."

"You ought to have a talk with Greeves, Uncle," said Bonnie. "He just sent Papa and the cubs away. Said you'd gone to a meeting in town."

The squire frowned. "He did? That's

odd." With his foot he pressed a button connected to a cord that ran under the table. A bell rang in the front hall, and soon Greeves appeared.

"Oh, you're still here, sir," said the butler with surprise.

"Of course I'm 'still' here," said Squire Grizzly. "Why did you tell Papa I'd left?"

"Well," said Greeves, "I knew you had that meeting this morning, sir, and I saw the chauffeur leave."

"That meeting is *tomorrow* morning, Greeves!" said the squire.

"Oh, I'm terribly sorry, sir," said the butler. "I'm getting so forgetful. My head's been spinning from all those sleepless nights lately."

"But you look well rested today," said the squire.

"Only on the outside, sir," said Greeves.

"On the inside, I'm a wreck."

"Oh, all right," said Squire Grizzly. "You can go now, Greeves."

"Thank you, sir."

When the butler had gone, Squire Grizzly turned to Papa and said, "Well, what about that chair, Papa? Don't tell me it's already fixed!"

"I won't," said Papa. "Because it isn't."

"But can you fix it?"

"I'm not sure how to break this to you, Squire," said Papa. "There's good news and bad news."

"What's the good news?" asked the squire.

"The good news is that the chair will be easy to fix," said Papa.

"Fine," said the squire. "Then fix it. What's the bad news?"

"The bad news," said Papa, "is that the chair's a fake."

"It's a *what?*" said the squire.

"A fake," Papa repeated. "A cleverly made copy. Brand-new."

"That means we've been *robbed!*" cried the squire, pounding the table. "But when? How? And by *whom?*"

THAT MEANS WE'VE BEEN <u>ROBBED</u>!

Chapter 8
Rudely Awakened

"I'll bet the ghosts did it!" said Sister. "The ones Maisie saw!"

"What have they done?" said a voice from the entranceway to the dining room. "And who was robbed?"

It was Lady Grizzly. She was wearing a nightgown with a robe over it. She looked exhausted.

"I thought you were asleep, dear," said Squire Grizzly.

"I was finally dozing off," said Lady Grizzly, "when I heard someone shout the word *robbed* and bang the dining room table."

"Oh...er...that was me, dear," said the squire sheepishly.

"Never mind that," said Lady Grizzly. "Who was robbed?"

The squire gave Papa a glance and said, "I'm not sure how to break this to you, dear. There's good news and bad news."

"Tell me the bad news first," said Lady Grizzly.

"The bad news is that I sat in your favorite rosewood chair and broke it."

"Oh, dear!" cried Lady Grizzly. "Didn't I tell you to go on a diet? But what's the good news?"

"The good news," said the squire, "is that the chair I broke isn't really your favorite rosewood chair after all."

"I don't understand," said Lady Grizzly. "What is it, then?"

"It's...er...a fake," said the squire.

"A *fake?*" cried Lady Grizzly. "That's not good news. That's *terrible* news! We've been robbed!" She fell back into a chair. "Check all the furniture in the west wing immediately! Oh, my beautiful antiques!"

Papa and the squire hurried off. They were gone several minutes. When they returned, they had gloomy expressions on their faces.

"Bad news," moaned Lady Grizzly. "I can tell."

Papa nodded. "It's not just the rosewood chair," he said. "A dozen of the oldest and most valuable antiques in the west wing have been replaced with fakes."

Chapter 9
Ghostly Logic

Lady Grizzly could hardly speak. Her breathing came in short bursts. Finally, she cried, "My collection is *ruined!*"

Squire Grizzly hurried to her side. He took her hand in his and patted it. "Don't worry, dear," he said. "We'll catch these burglars and get your antiques back!"

"No, we won't," moaned Lady Grizzly.

"But why not, dear?" said the squire.

"Because we can't catch *ghosts!*" wailed Lady Grizzly.

"Oh, Auntie," said Bonnie. "It wasn't ghosts who stole your antiques."

"That's easy for you to say, dear," said

Lady Grizzly, drying her eyes with a handkerchief. "You probably don't even believe in ghosts."

"You're right," said Bonnie. "I *don't* believe in ghosts. But the ghosts I don't believe in would never bother to replace stolen antiques with fakes. They'd just take them. You yourself just said that we can't catch ghosts. But whoever switched the antiques with fakes did it so no one would know the antiques were missing. And why? Because they were *afraid of being caught*."

The dining room was silent as everyone thought about what Bonnie had said.

"She does have a point, dear," said the squire to his wife.

"Indeed, she does," said Lady Grizzly. She looked surprised. "In fact, she's absolutely right. I *do* believe in ghosts. But the ghosts I believe in would act exactly the same way that the ghosts Bonnie *doesn't* believe in would act!"

"Huh?" said the squire, with a puzzled look. "Oh, never mind. At least we all agree that the burglars are not ghosts."

Everyone but Sister Bear, that is. Sister still wasn't convinced. Especially after that nightmare she'd had the night before. But it wasn't only the nightmare. It was Farnsworth Grizzly's eyes following her from his portrait. And something else was just as puzzling...

"But what about Maisie?" Sister said. "How do you explain what she saw in the ballroom? She couldn't have imagined it all. That would be too much of a coincidence."

Everyone thought hard. It was a tough question.

Finally, Bonnie said, "I've got it. Maisie really did see the burglars that night. But she just *imagined* that they were dressed like Bad Bart and his men. And her imagination turned their flashlight into a candle, too."

"Yeah," said Brother. "Her imagination turned real burglars into ghosts because she already believed that the mansion was haunted!"

Everyone liked the idea. Even Sister had to admit that Bonnie had come up with a pretty good explanation. "It could be true," she said.

"Of course it's true!" said Squire Grizzly. "Any explanation *that* good *deserves* to be true!"

THE BUTLER DID IT!

Chapter 10
Tillie's Tale

"Well," said Lady Grizzly, "if we all agree that ghosts didn't steal my antiques, then who did?"

The room was silent again. No one seemed to have any ideas.

"There must be a carpenter involved," said Papa finally. "One who got a good close-up look at the antiques. I don't know of any carpenter who could make such fine copies from drawings or photographs."

"But the carpenter may not have been in on the burglary," said Lady Grizzly.

"Hmm," said Papa. "A good point, Lady Grizzly. The burglars could have taken the antiques to the carpenter and paid him to copy them without his ever knowing they were stolen."

"If that's what happened, I can find out in minutes," said Lady Grizzly. "Make a list of the stolen items, Papa. I shall telephone every carpenter from Beartown to Big Bear City and ask them if they've made any of these copies."

Papa made the list and gave it to Lady Grizzly, who hurried off to her east wing study.

"I just thought of something," said Squire Grizzly. "It must have been very tricky getting those antiques out of the mansion and those copies into it. Someone inside the mansion must have helped the burglars!"

"That's easy," said Bonnie. "I've been in lots of mystery plays, and you know what always happens in them. *The butler did it!*"

"Greeves?" gasped Squire Grizzly. "Impossible! Greeves has been with us for thirty-five years. He is one of our most loyal and trusted servants."

"What about his strange behavior lately?" said Bonnie.

"His forgetfulness?" said the squire. "Everyone's forgetful from time to time. Especially when they're tired."

"I guess you haven't heard Tillie's story," said Bonnie. "Maybe you should ring her."

The squire rang for the housekeeper.

EARLY IN THE MORNING I SAW HIM DRIVE OFF IN HIS CAR . . .

Moments later she appeared. "You rang, sir?" she said.

"Tillie," said Bonnie, "please tell my uncle what you told me about Greeves a few days ago."

"Yes, miss," said Tillie. "Well, sir, it happened on Greeves's day off nearly two weeks ago. Early in the morning I saw him drive off in his car. He was wearing ordinary clothes. But a few minutes later he was back in uniform again, standing in the front hall. He said he'd almost forgotten that the exterminators were arriving that morning. They were supposed to get rid of the mice in the old cellar under the west wing. Now, here's the odd thing about it, sir. The very next morning, when I asked him if the exterminators were finished in the west wing, he said, 'What exterminators?' He didn't remember returning to the mansion to let them in."

"Hmm," said Squire Grizzly. "That certainly is odd."

"That's not all, sir," said Tillie. "Greeves remembered all about the exterminators later. This morning I heard him use the intercom in the front hall to tell the security guard that they were coming back today."

"Hmm," said the squire once more. "Thank you, Tillie. You may go." With a curtsy, Tillie left the room.

"Well, Uncle," said Bonnie, "is that strange enough for you?"

"It's stranger than you think," said the squire.

"Why is that?" asked Papa.

"Because," said the squire, "neither Lady Grizzly nor I ever told Greeves to call the exterminators."

Chapter 11
To the West Wing!

"I'll bet those exterminators are crooks!" said Bonnie. "And Greeves is helping them!"

Squire Grizzly looked stunned. "I just can't believe that," he said. "I'll ring Greeves and give him a chance to explain all this."

The squire rang for the butler and waited. But no one came. He rang again. And again and again. Still Greeves didn't appear.

"Greeves!" roared the squire. "Where are you? I must speak with you!"

Still no answer.

"He's probably in the west wing, stealing more furniture!" said Bonnie.

Squire Grizzly dashed to the intercom on the wall and pressed a button. "Harris?" he said.

"Yes, sir?" said the front gate's guard.

"Have the exterminators arrived yet?"

"The Bug Bears?" said the guard. "Yes, sir. About half an hour ago. They drove their van around to one of the side doors of the west wing. Greeves was going to meet them there."

"And they're still here?"

"Yes, sir," said Harris.

"Now listen carefully, Harris," said the squire. "Close and lock the front gate. Call the other guards on your walkie-talkie and tell them to lock their gates, too. Let no one leave the grounds until I say so. Got that?"

"Yes, sir," said Harris. "Right away, sir."

Squire Grizzly looked off in the direction of the west wing. His eyes blazed with fury. "Greeves, that traitor!" he snarled.

Hanging on the wall was a row of riding crops. The squire took two of them down and handed one to Papa. "Let's go get him, Papa!" he cried. "Him and those phony exterminators! To the west wing!"

Off ran Squire Grizzly, waving his riding crop.

Sister grabbed Papa's arm. "Don't go, Papa!" she pleaded. "It could be danger-ous!"

"The squire's out of control!" said Papa. "I've got to protect him! Stay here, cubs!"

And off he ran after Squire Grizzly.

Chapter 12
The Grandfather's Clock

Meanwhile, in her east-wing study, Lady Grizzly was talking on the phone to a carpenter in Big Bear City. Papa's list lay before her on her desk. Against the wall behind her stood her favorite antique grandfather's clock.

Usually the peaceful ticking of the old clock and the swinging of its great pendulum were soothing to Lady Grizzly. But right now she was too upset to be soothed by anything.

"Oh, I'm so glad you're in, Mr. Bevel," she said into the phone. "I wonder if you've recently made a copy of a Bruin Phyfe rosewood chair? No?" She ran her finger down the list. "What about a Chippenbear drop-leaf table?"

Lady Grizzly was concentrating so hard on her list that she didn't notice that the grandfather's clock had stopped ticking. It had stopped ticking because its pendulum had stopped swinging. And that was because a gloved hand had reached out from inside the wall behind the clock and grabbed the pendulum!

Now the hand carefully drew the pendulum to one side as another hand pushed open the long, narrow glass door of the clock. Moments later the clock began ticking again.

Lady Grizzly continued reading the list of items. She had no idea that someone had slipped into the room through the grandfather's clock and was tiptoeing toward her.

"I want to thank you for your patience, Mr. Bevel," Lady Grizzly said. "There's just one more item on the list. It's a—"

She never finished her sentence. A gloved hand had clapped itself over her mouth.

Struggling with all her might, Lady Grizzly was dragged across the room and into the grandfather's clock. Then the glass door of the clock was pulled shut from within.

Once again the great clock ticked peacefully away in the empty room.

On the desk lay the phone, talking to no one. "Hello? Hello?" it said. "Lady Grizzly, are you still there...?"

Chapter 13
In the Old Library

Riding crop held high, Squire Grizzly crept into the old library of the west wing. He had heard a noise there. Could it be the burglars?

"Squire!" came Papa Bear's voice from the direction of the ballroom. "Squire! Where are you?"

But the squire didn't answer. He was staring at a shelf filled with books. Hadn't he just heard a *clunk* behind it?

Squire Grizzly tiptoed to the bookshelf. He listened. Another clunk. He leaned toward the shelf until his ear was almost touching the books...

All of a sudden the bookshelf folded inward and disappeared into the wall! Two arms shot out of the black space, grabbed Squire Grizzly around the neck, and pulled him in!

Back into place swung the bookshelf.

In the ballroom, Papa was getting worried. "Squire Grizzly?" he called again. "Are you all right?"

The only room in the west wing that Papa hadn't checked yet was the old library. So he went in and looked around. There was no one there. Nothing but rows and rows of dusty old books.

"Hmm," Papa said to himself. "Maybe the squire didn't come in here."

Papa suddenly felt very tired. After all, he had looked all over the west wing. He decided to rest for a few seconds before going on with his search.

He noticed a comfortable-looking chair against one of the library walls. *Better not,* he thought. He remembered what Squire Grizzly had done to one chair already. But his feet ached. *I'll be extra careful,* he thought.

The moment Papa sat down, the wall opened up behind him and swallowed the chair with him still in it. Seconds later the chair slid back out, and the wall closed again.

But the chair was empty!

Chapter 14
Bear Detective for a Day

In the east-wing dining room, the cubs strained to hear.

"Papa's not calling anymore," said Brother.

"He must have found Uncle Squire," said Bonnie.

"Either that," said Sister, "or something bad happened to him."

"Like what?" said Cousin Fred.

"Like maybe he was caught by the bur- glars," said Sister. She looked as if she might cry.

"You've got it backwards," said Fred. "Papa and the squire are trying to catch the burglars, not the other way around. And if I were a burglar and someone were trying to catch me, I'd run away."

"You're not a burglar," said Sister.

"No, and I'm not a *ghost,* either," said Fred.

"Knock off the arguing, guys," said Brother. "I think what we should do is call the police."

Brother dashed to the phone and called the police station. Deputy Hoskins answered and said that Chief Bruno and Officer Marguerite had taken the squad car to the other side of town. He would radio them right away, but it might take a while for them to get to Grizzly Mansion.

"I don't know if we can wait for them," said Sister. "I'm worried about Papa. Let's go look for him and the squire!"

"But Papa told us to stay here," said Brother.

"That's because he wants us to stay out of trouble," said Sister. "But what if *he's* in trouble?"

Brother looked from Sister to Fred to Bonnie. "Sister's right," he said. "We've got to do something. Bonnie, I'm making you a Bear Detective for the day."

Brother went to the wall and took down several riding crops. He passed them out to the cubs. "Defend yourselves if you have to," he said. "Let's go!"

Chapter 15
Picking Up the Scent

"Papa? Squire Grizzly?" the cubs called out as they stepped into the west wing of the mansion. But except for their own voices, there wasn't a sound.

"Now I *know* something's happened to them," said Sister.

"Come on. Let's check out the ballroom," said Brother. He and Bonnie and Cousin Fred made their way down the hall toward the ballroom.

Sister was left standing in the hall. Her feet just wouldn't move. She was scared to be left alone. But she was even more scared to go into that ballroom—the room where she had seen the ghosts of Bad Bart and his thieves.

Sister's heart pounded. Thoughts raced through her mind. First, she remembered that she hadn't *really* seen ghosts in the ballroom. That had just been a nightmare.

But then she remembered that Maisie *had* seen the ghosts. At least Maisie had thought so. But hadn't Bonnie explained that? And hadn't Squire Grizzly said her explanation was so good that it deserved to be true?

But Sister still wasn't convinced.

What finally did get Sister moving was her pride in being a Bear Detective. *The Bear Detectives never quit,* she reminded herself. *The Bear Detectives keep going until the case is solved.*

Sister tiptoed down the hall and into the ballroom. No one was there. She began to get scared again. Just then a cloud passed across the sun. Shadows crept through the great ballroom.

Sister stared at the row of suits of armor. She imagined one of them holding a candle. Then she imagined that the candle was *moving toward her...*

All of a sudden something brushed against Sister's shoulder. Instantly she turned, swinging her riding crop this way and that as hard as she could.

"Hey! Stop, Sis! It's me!"

Brother had his arms over his head, trying to shield it from Sister's attack.

"Don't sneak up on me like that!" snapped Sister.

HEY! STOP, SIS! IT'S ME!

"Sorry," said Brother. "We were in the old library when we realized you weren't with us. I came back to look for you."

"Well, you found me," said Sister. "Whew! I've got to sit down for a second. I feel a little dizzy."

"Come on with me," said Brother. "You can rest in the library."

Brother and Sister found Bonnie and Cousin Fred inspecting the bookcases.

"There's something weird about this," said Fred, pointing to one of the shelves. "All the books in this room are covered with dust—*except* for the ones on this shelf." He tried to pick one up. "It's stuck," he said. He tried some others. "They all are." He hit one to jar it loose. It made a funny sound. "They're hollow!" Fred said. "And they're attached to the shelf!"

Suddenly, the bookshelf folded into the wall, leaving a gaping black hole. At the very same moment, Sister disappeared into the opposite wall—along with the chair she'd just sat on!

But none of the other cubs noticed that Sister was gone. They were too busy staring into the hole in the wall where the bookshelf had been.

"What's in there?" said Fred.

"It's a stairway," said Brother, peering in.

"And it goes down. Maybe Papa and Squire Grizzly went down it. Let's go see!"

The three cubs climbed through the wall and started down the dark stairway.

"I hear pounding," said Bonnie.

"Maybe it's them!" said Brother.

But as they made their way down the stairs, the pounding seemed to get farther away.

That's because it was Sister Bear who was doing the pounding.

Chapter 16
Trapped!

Sister pounded the wall with her fists. "Hey! Let me out of here!" she yelled.

But no one came to help.

They're gone, she thought. *Now what'll I do? I'm trapped!*

Everything was pitch-black. Sister felt around her. Walls. A low ceiling. She must be in one of Farnsworth Grizzly's secret rooms! Was there a way out?

Suddenly her hand touched something on

the floor. It felt like a handle! She yanked at it. A door opened.

Peering down through the opening, Sister saw a dimly lit stairway. *A secret entrance to the old cellar,* she thought. The cellar must have some windows near the ceiling, she figured, or it would be pitch-black down there, too.

Should she go down? Her heart thumped against her ribs. She could almost hear ghosts creeping up those stairs...

Somehow Sister made her mind go blank. Slowly she stepped down the stairs. They went round and round in a spiral. Sister could barely breathe as she went. But at least there was enough light to see by.

At last she reached the bottom of the stairs. A long, dark tunnel stretched off before her. She walked down it, running her hand along the cool wall. Her heart

fluttered as a mouse scurried past.

Finally, Sister came to a spot where the tunnel made a sharp turn to the left. What was that sound around the corner? More mice? Or was it...*ghosts?*

Sister raised her riding crop just as three spooky figures jumped out from around the corner and began hitting her over the head. She screamed and struck back wildly. She had been right! The place *was* haunted! The ghosts screamed, too, as they swung at her with riding crops...

"Stop!" yelled Brother. "It's just Sister!"

The four cubs lowered their weapons and stood panting.

"Whew!" said Brother. "We thought you were a burglar, Sis."

"I thought *you* were burglars!" said Sister. She was too embarrassed to say what she had really thought.

Chapter 17
To the Rescue

"There's light coming from that direction," said Fred. He was pointing back down the tunnel. "Let's go check it out."

This time the cubs held hands to keep together. They made their way down the dimly lit tunnel as quickly as they could. The light at the end of the tunnel seemed to be coming from above. It fell on a clutter of large, dark objects.

"Furniture!" cried Brother.

"Auntie's stolen antiques!" said Bonnie. "The burglars must have stored them here."

Fred pointed to a wooden ladder that led up to a square of light near the ceiling. "The light's coming from that open cellar door," he said. "They must have got out that way."

Just then a thumping sound came from somewhere nearby.

"Or *in*," whispered Sister.

Another thump. And another.

Brother put a finger to his lips and pointed to a door just down the tunnel. With their crops raised, the cubs tiptoed toward it. Their hearts pounded.

Sister's knees shook so much, she could hardly walk. She kept telling herself that she didn't believe in ghosts. But deep down, she was still terrified that the burglars would turn out to be the ghosts of Bad Bart and his band of thieves.

As the cubs neared the door, they heard a new sound.

"Shhh!" said Brother.

"Voices," whispered Fred.

"Voices *moaning and groaning*," whispered Bonnie.

"That's it," said Sister. "I'm outta here!"

Sister turned to run, but Brother grabbed her by the arm. "You know I don't believe in ghosts, Sis," he said. "But the ghosts I don't believe in don't moan and groan like that."

"They d-d-don't?" said Sister.

"No," said Brother. "Real live bears who are bound and gagged moan and groan like that! Let's go!"

Sure enough, inside the old storage room

were three bears all tied up. Pieces of cloth were fastened tightly around their mouths. The bears were Lady Grizzly, Squire Grizzly, and Papa Bear.

The cubs untied them by the light from a little square window near the ceiling.

"Greeves!" bellowed Squire Grizzly the moment the gag was out of his mouth. "He and his phony exterminators! They tied us up!"

"See?" said Bonnie. "I *told* you the butler did it."

"That traitor!" growled the squire. "When

I get my hands on him—"

A loud thump interrupted the squire. "What was that?" he said.

"It's coming from that wall," said Papa. "There must be a hidden room behind it."

And indeed there was. On one wall of the old storage room Brother found a button. He pressed it, and a hidden door slid open.

The light from the storage room fell across another figure that was bound and gagged. He lay on the rough cellar floor, dressed only in pajamas.

Squire Grizzly let out a gasp. "Greeves!"

Chapter 18
The Butler's Tale

"I don't understand," said Lady Grizzly, peering in at the butler. "Why would Greeves tie *himself* up?"

"For heaven's sake, dear!" said Squire Grizzly. "He didn't tie himself up!"

"Then who did?" said Lady Grizzly.

"Isn't it obvious?" said the squire. "He and his partners must have had an argument—probably about who would get the biggest share of the money when they sold the stolen antiques. So they tied him up and left him behind."

By now the cubs had untied Greeves.

"That's not what happened!" cried the butler. "I had nothing to do with the burglary!"

"Then why did you and your partners

tie us up!" said Squire Grizzly.

"We didn't!" said Greeves. "I mean, *I* didn't! I mean, they're not my partners! I don't even know *who* tied you up!"

"*You* did!" roared the squire. "I looked you right in the eye while you did it!"

"But I've been down here since before dawn!" said Greeves. "The ghosts attacked me while I was still in bed! They tied me up and dragged me down here! I was terrified!"

"Did you say *ghosts?*" said Lady Grizzly.

"Yes!" said Greeves. "The same ones Maisie saw in the ballroom last week!"

Just then a police siren wailed above-ground.

"I won't allow you to hide behind this ghost nonsense!" Squire Grizzly said to the butler. "Get up! We're turning you over to Chief Bruno!"

Chapter 19
Which One?

After all that time in the dim cellar, the bears had to shield their eyes from the bright sunlight as they came out.

"Aha!" said Squire Grizzly. "Here's the getaway van!"

It was pulled up close to the cellar door. On its side was printed THE BUG BEARS in big letters. Smaller letters below said *We Do Mice, Too!*

Just then Chief Bruno came walking around the corner of the mansion. Tillie and Maisie were with him.

"Greeves?" said Tillie, staring hard at the butler. "Is that you? What in the world are you doing in your pajamas?"

"My wife's antiques have been stolen, Chief," said Squire Grizzly. "And we've caught the head burglar!"

"The butler did it," said Bonnie.

"No, I didn't!" said Greeves.

"*I* believe him, Chief," said Lady Grizzly. "The mansion is haunted! The ghosts of Bad Bart Grizzly and his band of thieves have made off with a dozen of my antiques!"

"*I* saw them stealing one," said Maisie.

"And they tied *me* up!" said Greeves.

"Nonsense!" roared Squire Grizzly. "His partners tied him up, Chief! And *he* tied *us* up!"

"Then why is he in his pajamas, dear?" asked Lady Grizzly. "He was in uniform when he tied us up. Why would they make him get into his pajamas just to tie him up?

I believe he *was* attacked while he was still in bed, just as he says."

"What are you talking about, dear?" said the squire.

"And another thing," said Lady Grizzly. "When Greeves tied us up, he had no bags under his eyes. But look at him now. The bags are back!"

"But you yourself just said that *he* tied us up!" cried the squire.

"Oh, dear," said Lady Grizzly. "I did, didn't I? Now I'm confused..."

"You're not the only one," said Chief Bruno. "What *I* want to know is where those so-called Bug Bears are. If we find *them,* I think we might be able to solve this crime."

Just then Bonnie pointed across the lawn toward the west gate and said, "I'll bet that's them!"

Everyone turned to look. Walking toward them in a row were three bears. They were all handcuffed. Behind them marched Officer Marguerite with her pistol drawn. Two of the bears wore uniforms with BUG BEAR printed across the front. The third had on a different kind of uniform. A *butler's* uniform.

"I caught your butler and these two jokers trying to escape through a tunnel under your fence," Officer Marguerite told Squire Grizzly. "They look pretty guilty to me. Case solved."

But was it? Everyone looked from the

bear in the butler's uniform to the bear in pajamas, then back to the bear in the uniform. There was Greeves in his pajamas, standing next to Lady Grizzly. And *there* was Greeves in his uniform, standing next to the Bug Bears.

"I still think the butler did it," said Bonnie, her eyes wide. "I'm just not sure *which one!*"

Chapter 20
The *Other* Butler's Tale

Greeves One and Greeves Two. There they stood. But how could there be two of them?

Greeves in butler's uniform smiled at Greeves in pajamas and said, "Hello, Greeves." It was Greeves's voice. It sounded just like the butler talking to himself.

"Oh, my goodness!" shrieked Lady Grizzly. "It's Greeves's *ghost!*" She nearly fainted, but the squire caught her and held her up.

"That is no ghost, madam," said Greeves in pajamas, looking straight at Greeves in uniform. Again, it was Greeves's voice "*That*...is my long-lost twin brother, Arthur!"

Greeves in uniform just smiled.

"Long-lost twin brother?" said Squire Grizzly. "I didn't know you had a twin brother, Greeves."

"I'd nearly forgotten all about him myself," said Greeves. "As a teenager, he ran away from home and joined the navy. Neither I nor anyone else in the family has heard from him in forty years. All that time we've had no idea where he was or what he was doing."

"You'd better start explaining," Chief Bruno said to Arthur. "If you cooperate, the judge might take a few months off that long prison sentence he's sure to give you and your partners."

Arthur looked at the Bug Bears and muttered, "Lucky us." Then he turned back to the others. "Oh, all right," he said. "It's a long story. When I got out of the navy, I settled way up north in Polar Bear City and became an assistant to a carpenter there. Soon I had my own carpentry business and these two assistants, Chuck and Charlie." He nodded at the Bug Bears. "The exterminators' van here is really our business van. We repainted it for this...er...*job*."

Papa Bear was listening with widening eyes. "Do you mean to say that you three made the copies of Lady Grizzly's antiques?" he asked.

Arthur's smile showed more than a hint of pride. "Exactly," he said.

"But how did you find out where *I* was?" asked Greeves.

"From an article about Squire Grizzly in

the *Polar Gazette*," said Arthur. "He had just given a lot of money to charity. Next to the article was a photograph of the squire and Lady Grizzly being served tea in Grizzly Mansion—by *you*. Though I hadn't seen you in forty years, I recognized you instantly."

That's not surprising, thought Sister Bear as she looked from one twin to the other. They were the same height and weight, and they had the same faces and voices. The only difference between them was that one was wearing a butler's uniform and the other was wearing pajamas.

Well, not the only difference. When Sister looked more closely, she noticed that the twin in pajamas had bags under his eyes, but that the twin in the butler's uniform didn't.

"Of course, as a carpenter, I already knew

all about Lady Grizzly's famous antique collection," continued Arthur. "I began to work on a scheme to get ahold of some of those priceless antiques by posing as Greeves. First I went to the history section of the public library and read up on Grizzly Mansion. That's how I found out about the secret tunnels and cellars that old Farnsworth Grizzly built under and around the mansion. They sounded like perfect places to set up a woodworking shop for a couple of weeks."

"You made the copies down there?" gasped Squire Grizzly. *"Right under our noses?"*

"Of course," said Arthur. "It would have been far too risky going back and forth, taking antiques out of the mansion and bringing copies in. We needed to be inside the mansion so we could switch antiques and

copies over a long period of time. Then, once we were done, we could take the antiques out all at once.

"So we tunneled under the back fence and broke into the old cellar. We wasted no time in using the secret tunnels in the walls on the upper floors to spy on the household. The tunnels ran right behind portraits of Grizzly forebears. Very convenient. We just cut flaps in the portraits' eyes and spied through them. After a day of spying, we'd learned everything we needed to know.

"The most important thing we learned was when Greeves's next day off would be. As soon as he left, I sneaked into his room, put on his uniform, and buzzed the guard at the front gate to tell him to expect the Bug

Bears. Meanwhile, my friends here had slipped out through the tunnel under the fence and gone to get our van. So, in they came, right through the front gate, carrying all our woodworking equipment along with plenty of lumber and a supply of canned foods. After unloading everything into the cellar, out they went again through the front gate."

"So *that's* why you didn't remember about the exterminators!" said Tillie to Greeves. "Because it wasn't you who called them in. It was Arthur!"

"I thought Tillie here might get suspicious about that and come snooping in the west wing if she heard us moving furniture at night," said Arthur. "So we prepared for that."

"What do you mean, *prepared for it?*" asked Chief Bruno.

94

Just then Officer Marguerite, who had gone to check the van, came back carrying a pile of clothing. "Found these in the van," she said, holding them up. "Some sort of costumes. The tags say BIG BEAR CITY COSTUME AND NOVELTY SHOP."

Maisie gasped. "That's what the ghosts in the ballroom were wearing!" she cried. "Old-fashioned highway robber outfits!"

"Well, it turned out that Tillie never came snooping," Arthur continued. "But Maisie did. While we were spying, we heard all about the ghosts. So I sent Charlie to Big Bear City to get costumes. I knew that if

any of the servants saw us dressed like that at night they'd be too scared to ever come snooping again."

"And he was right!" said Maisie to Chief Bruno. Tillie and Greeves nodded in agreement.

"I thought the candle was a nice touch, too," said Arthur. "We did all our work by candlelight, in fact. Each night we inspected an antique, copied it, and replaced the original with the copy. By last night we were done. We put on our 'ghost' costumes, gathered the antiques and our equipment near the cellar door, and waited.

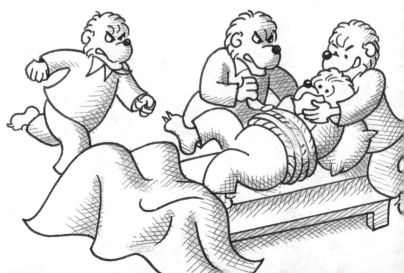

"Just before dawn we tied Greeves up. Then I put on his uniform. I made sure that the Bug Bears were let in the front gate again and told them to start loading the antiques and equipment into the van.

"That's when Papa Bear and the cubs arrived. I knew they'd been here the day before, and I was worried that Papa might discover that the rosewood chair was a fake. But I hoped he wouldn't find out in time to catch us."

"So that's why you turned us away," said Papa to Greeves. Then he frowned and said, "I didn't mean *you*, Greeves. I meant *Arthur*."

"Of course," said Arthur. "You told me someone had stolen one of Lady Grizzly's antiques. I couldn't let you tell the squire that, could I? At that point my helpers had just begun loading the antiques into the van. When I saw Bonnie bring Papa and the cubs into the mansion, I hurried to the west wing and told Chuck and Charlie to empty the van and help me spy on all of you.

"When Papa and Squire Grizzly went looking for us in the west wing, we knew our only chance was to tie them up and force our way out the front gate. We nabbed Lady Grizzly, too, because we were afraid she'd call the police. But before we could load the van, we heard a siren. We left the van and ran for the back fence. End of story."

"Forgot about us cubs, didn't you?" said Bonnie.

"We didn't *forget* about you," sniffed Arthur. "We never even thought about you."

"But that's *not* the end of the story," said Greeves angrily. "I want to know *why* you did it, Arthur."

"I wanted to be a millionaire like Squire Grizzly," said Arthur. "I wanted to have lots of money and live in a mansion. Don't you?"

"I *do* live in a mansion," said Greeves.

"Only as the butler," sneered Arthur.

At that, Greeves puffed out his chest. "Better as an honest butler than a crooked millionaire," he said proudly.

"Right, Greeves," said Squire Grizzly, giving the butler a pat on the back. "I owe you an apology. I should never have accused you of stealing."

"It's not your fault, sir," said Greeves. He pointed a finger at his twin brother. "It's *his* fault. Officer Marguerite, take these crooks away and lock them up!"

"I'll handle this, Greeves," said Chief Bruno. "Officer Marguerite, take these crooks away and lock them up!"

Chapter 21
A Grand Ball

Three important decisions were made as a result of what came to be known as the Great Antique Robbery.

The first was made by the judge of the Beartown court. He decided that Arthur and his assistants should spend twenty years in Bear Country Prison. They had committed not just one crime but several: they had broken into Grizzly Mansion; they had lived there without permission; they had attacked and tied up residents and visitors; and they had attempted to commit burglary.

That's right: they had *attempted* to commit burglary. One of the strangest facts about the entire story was that no burglary ever really happened. That's because the antiques were never actually removed from the Grizzly property.

The second decision was made by Squire Grizzly. He decided not to go on the diet that Lady Grizzly had been nagging him about. When she asked him why not, he said that if he *had* gone on that diet, the rosewood chair wouldn't have broken when he sat on it. If the chair hadn't broken, it wouldn't have been given to Papa Bear to be fixed. And if it hadn't been given to Papa Bear to be fixed, none of the fake antiques would have been discovered in time to catch the crooks! Lady Grizzly wasn't very pleased with her husband's decision. But after having lost so much sleep, she was too worn out to argue with him.

All Beartown, however, was very pleased with the third decision. Squire and Lady Grizzly decided to celebrate the return of Lady Grizzly's priceless antiques by throwing a big party—a grand ball—in the ballroom of the west wing of Grizzly Mansion. And Papa Bear was to be the official guest of honor. That's because his sharp carpenter's eye had kept Lady Grizzly's antiques from being stolen.

On the evening of the grand ball, the Bear family got into their car and headed for Grizzly Mansion. The butler greeted them at the front door.

Papa frowned. "Greeves?" he said. "Is that you?"

"Of course it's me, sir," said Greeves. "Who else would it be?"

"For a second," said Papa with a grin, "you looked just like Arthur."

Everyone laughed at Papa's joke. Then Greeves invited the Bears in. But Sister held back.

"What's wrong, Sis?" asked Brother.

Sister was standing straight and stiff on the welcome mat. Her eyes looked frightened. In her mind, she saw a gloomy ballroom filled with long shadows, floating candles, and walking suits of armor.

Greeves knelt beside Sister. "Still worried about ghosts in the ballroom?" he asked gently.

"I don't believe in ghosts," said Sister. She paused. She seemed to be holding something back. Then she took a deep breath and added, "But the ghosts I don't believe in still scare me sometimes when I think about them."

"I don't believe in ghosts anymore, either," said Greeves. "Not after what happened here at Grizzly Mansion."

"Then you think the ballroom is safe?" asked Sister.

"Very safe," said Greeves. "Because the ghosts I don't believe in would never haunt a ballroom filled with bears and music and bright lights. They'd wait until the dark of night when the ballroom was empty— empty, that is, except maybe for one lonely, frightened bear."

Sister shivered. But at the same time she smiled. "You're right, Greeves," she said firmly. "I feel better already."

"Excellent," said the butler. "Now I suggest you all go into the ballroom and have a wonderful time."

And that's exactly what they did. Even Sister.

Stan and Jan Berenstain began writing and illustrating books for children in the early 1960s, when their two young sons were beginning to read. That marked the start of the best-selling Berenstain Bears series. Now, with more than one hundred books in print, videos, television shows, and even Berenstain Bears attractions at major amusement parks, it's hard to tell where the Bears end and the Berenstains begin!

Stan and Jan make their home in Bucks County, Pennsylvania, near their sons—Leo, a writer, and Michael, an illustrator—who are helping them with Big Chapter Books stories and pictures. They plan on writing and illustrating many more books for children, especially for their four grandchildren, who keep them well in touch with the kids of today.